DRAGON HEROES

Adapted by Natalie Shaw

Ready-to-Read

Simon Spotlight

New York   London   Toronto   Sydney   New Delhi

SIMON SPOTLIGHT

An imprint of Simon & Schuster Children's Publishing Division

1230 Avenue of the Americas, New York, New York 10020

This Simon Spotlight edition August 2020

DreamWorks Dragons © 2020 DreamWorks Animation LLC. All Rights Reserved.

All rights reserved, including the right of reproduction in whole or in part in any form.

SIMON SPOTLIGHT, READY-TO-READ, and colophon are registered trademarks of Simon & Schuster, Inc.

For information about special discounts for bulk purchases, please contact Simon & Schuster Special Sales at 1-866-506-1949 or business@simonandschuster.com.

Manufactured in the United States of America 0720 LAK

10 9 8 7 6 5 4 3 2 1

ISBN 978-1-5344-7670-7 (hc)

ISBN 978-1-5344-7669-1 (pbk)

ISBN 978-1-5344-7671-4 (eBook)

Unlike most humans,
twins Dak and Leyla
can speak with dragons!
Together with their dragons,
Summer and Winger,
they help humans and
dragons in danger.

One day during a storm,
they rescued a human!
His name was Chief Duggard.

He was the chief of an island
called Huttsgalor.
He did not know that humans
and dragons could be friends
or could speak to each other!

"When we were little,
a mother dragon rescued us,"
Leyla told Duggard.

She and Dak were raised
by a mother dragon who
taught them to speak dragon.
"We also learned how
to ride them," Dak said.

"Amazing!" Duggard said.
Then he asked for
a ride home!

People on the island of
Huttsgalor were scared
of dragons.

But they also needed help.
After the big storm, their
village was wet and messy.
The blacksmith could not
even light a fire
because her oven was wet.

And her oven is how
she fixes things!
"Maybe we can help!"
Dak said.

Winger blew warm air
to dry out the oven.

Burple loaded it with coal.

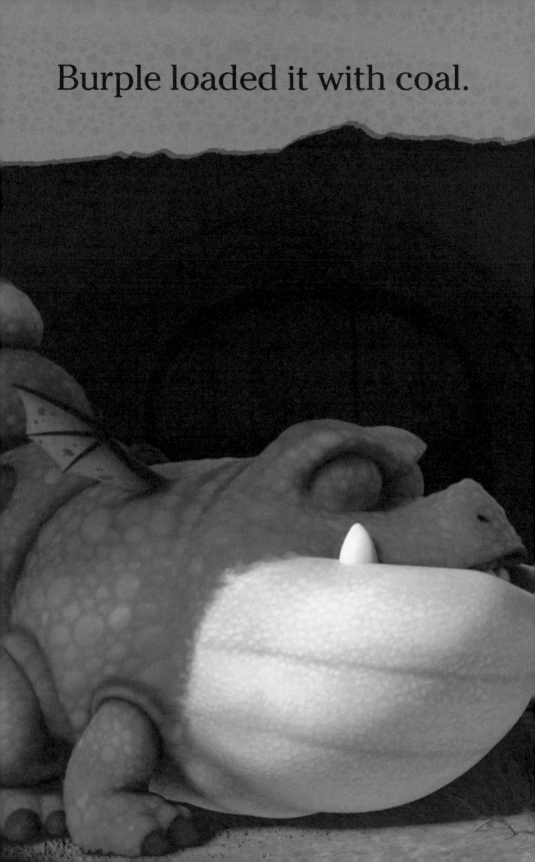

Cutter took a deep breath.
Then he lit the coals
with fire!

"Thank you!"
the blacksmith said.

Chief Duggard asked if they could stay to help more.

Cutter could cut trees
to help repair the roofs
that were damaged
in the storm.

But a villager named Magnus
did not want the dragons
to help.

He wanted people to use a machine he made to cut down trees.

The machine was fast.

Cutter was faster!

So Magnus made the machine go faster too.

Logs began to fly out
of the machine
and all over the village!

Dak, Leyla, and the dragons came to the rescue!

When it was all over,
Chief Duggard asked them
to stay again.
He gave them the lighthouse
as a home.

And he gave them
a new name.
"Rescue Riders," he said.
"I like it!" said Dak.

Now the Rescue Riders
have a home on the island.
And they still help
anyone, dragon or human,
who needs them.